This book b[elongs to] D1632292

_____

A catalogue record for this book is available from the British Library

Published by Ladybird Books Ltd
80 Strand, London, WC2R 0RL
A Penguin Company

2 4 6 8 10 9 7 5 3 1
© LADYBIRD BOOKS LTD MMIX
LADYBIRD and the device of a Ladybird are trademarks of Ladybird Books Ltd

ISBN: 978-1409301-173-8

Printed in China

Five-minute Tales
Busiest Pirate Ever

written by Marie Birkinshaw
illustrated by Caroline Freake

Busy Pirate Billy

Busy Pirate Billy lives with his mum, Captain June, his dad, First Mate Ben, Spud, the ship's cook and Seaweed, the ship's cat. Their home is an amazing pirate ship, called the Goldrush. Every day they sail the seas in search of buried treasure.

Billy's best friend is Seaweed. Busy Pirate Billy is always busy on the Goldrush helping Captain June and having fun. Seaweed likes to sleep in the sun.

Early one morning, Billy got out of bed.
He put on his pirate clothes, and said,
"Come on, Seaweed. There's work to do.
But we must be quiet or we'll wake the crew."

He took out his telescope and looked at the sea… But the ship wasn't bobbing up and down as it should be. It was rushing towards the rocks at great speed!

Straightaway, the busy little pirate took charge. Ding, ding! He rang the ship's bell to wake everyone up.

"It's too early, Pirate Billy. Go back to sleep!" First Mate Ben yawned, and closed his eyes again.

Ding, ding! "We've lost the anchor!" Billy shouted. "All hands on deck!"
Captain June raced to the wheel and set the ship straight in the water.

"Well done, my busy Billy," said Captain June
"You saved the Goldrush!"
Billy grinned happily.

Spud and Billy got busy making the breakfast for the crew, and of course, Seaweed ate at the table, too.

The Pirate Games

Today was the Junior Pirate Games.
All the pirate families met up for an
exciting day of games for the young
pirates. Billy and Seaweed had been
busy practising for weeks.

As the Goldrush steered towards the island where the games were held, the busy little pirate watched through his telescope. "Come on, Seaweed," Billy said, "we've lots to do."

Junior Pirate Games

The first event of the Junior Pirate Games was diving for gold coins. Billy wore his lucky diving mask, but it started to come loose and filled with water. Seaweed dived in and tried to help, but his paw got caught in Billy's hair. Billy came fifth.

The second event was ship steering skills in the bay. "I should be good at this!" said Billy. But his Captain's hat came down over his eyes and he couldn't see properly, so Billy came fourth.

The next event was a treasure hunt where Billy had to find ten gold coins and put them in a chest.
Billy started to dig. He found eight gold coins, an old boot and a crisp packet.
He came third.

Play sword fighting followed. Swords flashed and metal clashed. Seaweed went to find somewhere to sleep. The busy little pirate did well and came second.

At last it was time for the final game – deck cleaning. When the judges checked the boards, Billy's were the cleanest of all. They were so shiny that Seaweed could use them as a mirror. He came first!

At the end of the day, Billy was the only junior pirate to finish all the events.
Billy won the prize of the The Busiest Pirate Ever! Even Seaweed got a prize for eating the most fish!

Busy Pirate Billy and the Mysterious Map

It was spring-cleaning day on the Goldrush. At sunrise, busy little Pirate Billy and Seaweed rang the ship's bell. Everyone groaned and gathered on the top deck.

"Right, crew," said Captain June.
"It's time to scrub and clean. Make the
Goldrush as spotless as it's ever been."
All the crew set to work.

Billy and Seaweed went to the very bottom of the ship. This was where the barrels of drinking water were kept. Atishoo! Atishoo! It was dusty but they soon got to work.

Billy's broom got caught between two barrels and he had to pull hard to get it free. Pop! Out came the broom knocking Billy and Seaweed over.
"Look, Seaweed! It's a map!" Billy shouted.

The busy little pirate and the ship's cat took the map straight to Captain June. "Wow!" she said. "I haven't seen this before."
Seaweed pointed to the X with his paw.

"Come on, Seaweed," Billy said. "Let's get busy! I wonder what we'll find if we follow the clues."
The map led them to an old, rusty key.
"Will it fit this chest?" said Billy. "Let me see."
Billy clutched the key and put it in the lock.

Inside the chest was a dusty old recipe for Shiver me timbers ice cream! Spud, the ship's cook, was very happy.
"Oh thank you, Billy! Let's make ice cream!" Spud exclaimed.

When spring-cleaning was over, Billy
served the ice cream to everyone.
It was delicious!
"Three cheers for Billy! The busiest little
pirate ever!" sang the happy crew.